Shannon Jett

Printed in the USA.

Contents

The Pony Teacher.....3

Back in the Saddle.....14

A Friend for Popcorn.....26

The New Girl.....39

A Barn Mystery.....49

The Pony Wish.....63

Never Give Up.....78

Homesick.....90

The Ugly Pony.....107

The Horse Show.....118

The Pony Teacher

Bella walked excitedly into the barn. She loved riding lesson days. They were her favorite days of the week.

Bella had been riding for several months. She loved horses. She loved the way they smelled. She loved their soft muzzles. She loved feeding them treats. She didn't even mind cleaning stalls! But riding was her favorite part.

Bella's teacher was Miss Mallory. She was very nice. She knew a lot about horses, and she liked to share it with Bella and the other kids who took lessons.

Bella always rode a pony named Cocoa. Cocoa was a bay pony, which meant she had a brown body and a black mane and tail. Cocoa was really sweet. She always listened to Bella. She stood quietly while being brushed, was easy to steer, had a smooth trot, and would stop as soon as Bella said, "Whoa." Bella loved Cocoa.

"Hi, Miss Mallory!" Bella said cheerfully. "Should I go get Cocoa out of her stall?"

"Hi, Bella! I actually have a surprise for you today. You're going to ride a different pony. His name is Snowflake."

Bella got a little nervous. "What about Cocoa? I think I'd rather just ride Cocoa."

"I'm sorry, Bella. Cocoa has a sore hoof. She needs a little break. She's going to be just fine, but you will have to ride Snowflake for a few weeks."

Bella thought about it. She didn't want to miss riding lessons for a few weeks. She wanted to keep riding. She decided to give Snowflake a try.

"His stall is the last one on the left. You can get him out and brush him," Miss Mallory told her.

Bella headed to Snowflake's stall. She opened the door. Snowflake was a little bigger than Cocoa. He was pure white, except for a big mud stain he had on his shoulder!

"Oh, Snowflake! You rolled in the mud! We better get you brushed."

Bella grabbed his halter and went into the stall. Cocoa always came over to Bella. Snowflake did not. He was very busy eating his hay. He didn't seem interested in Bella at all.

Bella struggled to get his halter on, but she finally did it. She led him into the cross ties so she could brush him and put his saddle on.

Bella picked up a curry comb. The curry would help get some of the mud off of Snowflake's neck. Cocoa always loved the curry comb.

As Bella curried Snowflake, he danced around in the cross ties. He didn't want to stand still.

"It's hard to get you clean when you're always moving," Bella told him.

Next, she tried to pick his feet. Cocoa was always very patient while Bella picked any rocks or mud from her hooves. Snowflake was not patient. He stomped around and made Bella hurry. Once, he almost stepped on her foot!

Finally, Bella had the pony all groomed and ready to go. Miss Mallory showed Bella where Snowflake's saddle and bridle were. Bella got the pony all tacked up and ready to ride. She grabbed her helmet and put it on.

She led Snowflake to the arena and asked him to stand near the mounting block. She climbed the mounting block and started to put her foot in the stirrup to get on. Snowflake stepped away quickly. Bella nearly lost her balance and fell over. She caught herself and grabbed Snowflake's reins before he walked away.

"Snowflake!" Bella scolded him grumpily.

She tried the mounting block again. This time, Snowflake didn't move away, and Bella put her foot in the stirrup. When she started to step into the saddle, she felt it slipping. The saddle was too loose! Snowflake had held his breath when Bella tightened the girth. That meant that when he let his breath out, the saddle was too loose.

Bella was getting frustrated. Miss Mallory came to help and tightened the saddle. Finally, Bella was ready to ride!

Bella walked Snowflake around the arena. When Miss Mallory told the students to stop, or halt, their horses, Bella pulled lightly on the reins and said, "Whoa." Snowflake didn't stop! He kept walking. Miss Mallory showed Bella how to hold the reins a little tighter so Snowflake would listen better.

Snowflake was very different from Cocoa. Bella had to hold the reins tighter. She had to think ahead. She had to be sure to give clear signals about what she wanted to do. Riding Snowflake was a lot of work.

Bella was excited when it was time to trot. She loved trotting on Cocoa. Cocoa had such a smooth, easy trot. She got ready and cued Snowflake to trot. She sat deep in the saddle and squeezed. Snowflake started his trot.

Bounce, bounce, bounce! Snowflake had a boingy, bouncy trot. Bella felt like she was wiggling all over the saddle just trying to stay on. Miss Mallory called encouraging instructions. Bella did not like Snowflake's trot. Bella really missed Cocoa.

Bella worked hard for the rest of her lesson. She started to figure out how to ride Snowflake a little better. She got more comfortable riding with short reins.

When she was done riding, she took the saddle and bridle off of Snowflake. She brushed him and offered him a treat. Cocoa loved peppermints. They were her favorite. She gave Snowflake a peppermint. He spit it out!

"Snowflake! You are a very odd pony," Bella told him.

Her next riding lesson went about the same way. Bella felt like Snowflake must not like her. Riding Snowflake was a lot of work. Bella was really missing Cocoa. She hoped Cocoa would get better soon.

Bella was getting ready for her third riding lesson on Snowflake. Max came over while she was brushing Snowflake.

"Oh! You are riding Snowflake? You are lucky. Snowflake is a great pony," Max told her.

Bella looked at him in surprise. "Really? I don't think he likes me very much. He is always being difficult. I miss Cocoa."

"I don't think he means to be difficult. He is just sensitive. He is young, so sometimes he gets a little nervous," Max said as he put a hand on Snowflake to help him relax. "He has sensitive skin, so he likes soft brushes the best."

Bella thought about the hard curry she had used. Maybe Snowflake didn't like the hard curry. Bella chose a soft-bristled brush. She brushed his coat gently. Snowflake closed his eyes and relaxed.

Miss Mallory walked by as the kids were getting saddles on their ponies.

"Hey guys! Bella, are you ready to try a little jumping today?"

Bella gulped. She didn't know if she wanted to jump Snowflake. She was excited to try jumping for the first time. She wished she could jump Cocoa instead.

Bella shared this with Max. Max just laughed. "Snowflake is a way better jumper than Cocoa. Cocoa hates jumping. You will have a much easier time jumping Snowflake than Cocoa. All you have to do is steer Snowflake toward the jump. He will take care of the rest."

Bella was starting to figure out Snowflake a little more. She knew she needed to triple-check his girth to make sure the saddle didn't slide. She knew she needed to hold the reins tight so she could tell Snowflake what she wanted him to do.

She was even getting better at riding his bouncy trot. He trotted faster than Cocoa. Bella had to admit that it was kind of fun to trot fast.

Miss Mallory set up a small jump. She gave the kids instructions on how to ask their ponies to jump. When it was Bella's turn, she was nervous. She wanted to believe Max. But what if Snowflake was difficult?

Bella had to be brave. She asked Snowflake to trot. She found the middle of the jump. She looked over the jump where she wanted to go. As she got close to the jump, she grabbed Snowflake's mane, just like Miss Mallory told her to do. Snowflake trotted up to the jump and jumped it smoothly. He landed softly on the other side and trotted away.

Miss Mallory and her friends cheered. Bella gave Snowflake a big scratch on his neck. Snowflake had been a good boy!

Bella got the chance to jump a few more times. Each time, Snowflake did exactly what Bella asked him to do. Snowflake made jumping easy. Snowflake was a star!

When she was done riding, Bella took off the saddle and brushed Snowflake using a soft brush. She wished she knew a special treat that Snowflake would like. Bella asked Max.

"I think he likes sugar cubes the best. There are some in the feed room," he answered.

Bella grabbed some sugar cubes from the feed room. She offered them to Snowflake. Crunch, crunch, crunch! Snowflake gobbled up the sugar cubes. He nodded his head as if he was saying, "Yum!" Snowflake rubbed his head on Bella's arm. It seemed like Snowflake wanted to be her friend!

"I'm sorry I didn't understand you right away. You are very different from Cocoa, but you are a nice pony, too," Bella told him. "I guess ponies are like people. They each have their own personalities."

"That's right," Miss Mallory said as she walked up to them. "Each pony has things they like and don't like. Just like people. Each pony can teach us something different. Cocoa had things to teach you when you were a new rider. Now that you have been riding a while, it is time to learn new things. Snowflake can teach you things that Cocoa can't. He will help you be a better rider."

"Thank you, Snowflake, for helping me. I want to be a better rider. And jumping with you is really fun!" Bella said as she gave Snowflake a hug.

Back in the Saddle

Harper dug through her bookbag. She had saved an apple from her lunch. She wanted to share it with one of the ponies at her riding lesson.

"Ah, here it is!" she exclaimed as she stood up and presented the apple to Zippy.

"Want a bite?" she asked him.

Zippy looked at her happily. She held the apple firmly in her hand and offered him a bite. With a loud crunch, Zippy took a big bite of apple. Harper offered him one more bite before setting the apple to the side.

"Let's save the rest for after our ride," she said. She continued getting ready for her lesson. She brushed Zippy's smooth coat and picked the mud from his hooves.

"Are you almost ready?" Harper's best friend, Zoey, asked.

"Almost. I just have to get the saddle and bridle," Harper answered.

"Me too. And don't forget our helmets!"

Harper and Zoey took riding lessons together every Monday after school. They both loved horses, and it was fun to ride them together. The riding stable had lots of nice horses that the girls got to ride.

Harper and Zoey led their horses to the indoor arena. Their teacher was finishing up another lesson. Their moms waved to them from the bleachers, where they could sit and watch.

"Hi girls!" said Miss Stephanie. "Make sure you check your girth and adjust your stirrups, then I will help you mount up."

Harper checked the girth on Zippy. The girth was like the belt that held the saddle in place. If it was loose, the saddle would slip. She tightened it and made sure the stirrups would fit her. She liked riding

Zippy. He had a fast, fun trot. He could be a little sneaky, but he was a good pony if you paid attention.

Miss Stephanie helped Harper and Zoey mount their ponies. She told them to warm up at the walk. The girls walked the ponies around the arena. They practiced steering around some cones. They walked over some poles. Finally, Miss Stephanie told them they could trot.

"Let's put your ponies next to the arena rail and gather your reins. When you feel in control, give a little squeeze and ask your ponies to trot," she told them.

Harper kept her eyes up. Miss Stephanie always told them to look ahead. She had a good grip on her reins. She kept her heels down.

"Trot, Zippy!" she clucked to him.

Zippy went into a fast trot. Harper posted up and down with the rhythm.

"Easy, boy. Not too fast." Harper gave a gentle tug on the reins. Zippy responded immediately by doing a slower trot.

"Good job, Harper. You have good control of Zippy, and he is listening well to you," Miss Stephanie praised.

Miss Stephanie had the girls do a pattern. They had to steer the horses at a trot around some cones.

Next, Miss Stephanie had the girls practice trotting side by side. This was hard! Zippy liked to go fast. Zoey's horse liked to trot slowly. Harper had to work hard to make Zippy do a slower trot. Zoey had to work hard to make her horse do a faster trot. Both girls were giggling as they tried to ride side by side.

"This is harder than it looks!" Harper told her mom as they trotted by the bleachers.

Finally, the girls slowed the ponies to a walk.

Plink, plop, plink. A light rain started to fall outside. They could hear it on the metal roof.

"I'm sure glad we have an indoor arena to ride in today, or we would be getting WET!" exclaimed Zoey.

"Me too," said Miss Stephanie. "Luckily, we are nice and dry and safe from the rain. Now let's get back to the trot."

Harper shortened her reins and asked for a trot. Zippy listened and trotted around the arena.

KA-BOOOOOMMMMM!

All of a sudden, a huge clap of thunder rattled the barn.

The thunder scared Zippy. He bolted forward and took off at a run. Harper tried to hang on. She remembered all the things Miss Stephanie had taught her. She tried to sit up. She tried to pull on the reins, but Zippy was going so fast. Harper lost her balance. She felt herself slipping. Then she fell to the ground.

It all happened so fast! One minute she was in the saddle. The next minute she was sitting in the sand. Her lip began to quiver. She tried to hold in her tears, but she couldn't. In no time at all, she was crying really hard.

Miss Stephanie reached her first. She helped Harper sit up and encouraged her. Her mom reached her next. Her mom gave her a big hug and told her she had been brave. They asked if anything hurt. Her shoulder kind of hurt, but it wasn't too bad. Slowly, Harper stood up. She decided to walk with her mom over to sit on the mounting block and catch her breath.

One of the older kids had caught Zippy. Zippy didn't look scared anymore. He walked over to Harper and put his nose on her back. Harper sniffled. She reached out and petted Zippy's forehead. She knew he didn't mean to do it, but her feelings were a little hurt that she had fallen off.

"Zippy was really scared of the thunder!" Zoey said. "I'm glad you're OK! That was scary!"

Harper nodded. It was very scary!

"Do you think you want to try to get back on?" Miss Stephanie asked.

Harper thought about it. She was a little scared to get back on. Miss Stephanie seemed to sense that. "Do you want to sit in the saddle, and I can just lead you around walking so you know you can do it?"

Harper considered this. She decided to be brave.

"Yes, let's do that," she decided.

Her mom helped her brush the sand off her pants. She climbed up the mounting block while Miss Stephanie held Zippy. Harper took a deep breath. She closed her eyes. She could do this!

Harper petted Zippy's mane as she put her foot in the stirrup and swung into the saddle. The saddle felt familiar, but there were butterflies swooping around in Harper's tummy. She was nervous in the saddle now.

"You're doing great!" Miss Stephanie told her. "I'm proud of you for getting back on. Take a deep breath and let it out sloooooowly."

Harper breathed in and exhaled slowly. It did make her feel better. She reached up and petted Zippy again. Miss Stephanie led her around walking. Harper was glad she had gotten back up on Zippy. She was proud of herself for being brave.

The ride was over, and by then the rain had stopped. Harper and Zoey took the saddles off their horses and brushed them. They said goodbye to Miss Stephanie and promised to see her next week.

All week long Harper thought about her ride. All week long she thought about how scary it had been when Zippy had spooked at the thunder. All week long Harper was nervous about her riding lesson.

She finally told her mom.

"Of course, Honey! I think it is totally normal to be scared. But you love horses.

So you just have to decide what is bigger–your fear, or your love of horses."

"My love of horses," Harper replied with no hesitation.

"Well, I think you should give riding another try. You can start slow and see how it feels," her mom said.

Harper agreed to try. At the next lesson, she told Miss Stephanie her plan. Miss Stephanie agreed to let her ride at her own pace.

"Even if I only want to walk?" Harper asked.

"Even if you only want to walk," Miss Stephanie assured her.

Harper put on a brave face and fastened her helmet. She was riding Brownie, who was always kind. Harper used to think Brownie was slow, but today she was glad.

Harper rode all around at the walk. She felt herself relax with Brownie's smooth, slow walk. She steered through cones. She played Red Light, Green Light with Zoey.

She even walked Brownie over poles. She was feeling much better about riding. She was less afraid, but she still didn't want to trot yet.

Zoey was trotting all around the arena on her horse. She looked like she was having fun.

"Are you sure you don't want to trot?" Miss Stephanie asked her.

Harper only shook her head. She wasn't ready yet.

Miss Stephanie set up two poles. She told Harper she could walk over them. She asked Zoey if she wanted to trot over them. Zoey squealed with delight. She was so excited. Harper was happy for her friend. She watched as Zoey got prepared. Zoey's face was determined. She trotted her pony right up to the poles like Miss Stephanie had told her. She grabbed some mane and trotted over the poles. Boing, boing! The poles made her horse take a giant step. Zoey giggled.

"That was really fun! It's so bouncy!" she laughed. Miss Stephanie had Zoey practice trotting over the poles several more times. She got better with practice. It looked like so much fun.

Just as the lesson was almost over, Harper made a decision.

"Miss Stephanie, can I try trotting?" she asked.

"Of course!" Miss Stephanie cheered. "I think that is a great idea."

Harper gathered her reins. She took a deep breath. She asked Brownie to trot. Brownie stepped into a smooth, slow trot. Harper trotted twice around the arena. She got more comfortable. Her smile got bigger. Harper was glad she had been brave. She loved riding horses!

She asked Brownie to halt and gave her a big scratch on the neck. "Thank you, Brownie, for helping me be brave. Miss Stephanie, if I'm feeling brave next week, can I trot some poles too?"

"You bet! I'm really proud of you. It is scary to fall off a horse. It can be really scary to get back on. You faced your fears and were really brave today."

"I'm glad I was brave," Harper said. "I love horses too much to be afraid!"

A Friend for Popcorn

Popcorn was a good pony. She was a good listener, and she was kind. Popcorn loved children, and she always tried to do what her children wanted her to do. She was brave on the trails. She could run fast or walk slow–whatever her rider wanted to do. She always won pretty ribbons at horse shows. Popcorn prided herself on always being the best pony possible. It made her happy to make her little riders happy.

Except lately, Popcorn wasn't very happy. The children in her family had outgrown her. They didn't come to braid her mane anymore. They didn't sneak out after dark to feed her cookies. They didn't take her riding down by the pond. They were too busy with school and sports. It made Popcorn sad.

Popcorn still loved her family very much. They still took good care of her. She always had hay to eat and fresh water. She wore a warm blanket in the winter and stood in front of a cool fan in the heat of summer. But she missed having small riders to take on adventures. She was a small pony, and her children had grown too big to ride her anymore.

"Poor Popcorn," said Annie one day when she came to feed Popcorn her breakfast before leaving for school. "I'm sorry we don't have time to ride you anymore. You are still a good pony."

Popcorn enjoyed being called a good pony, but she wished they could go back to the days of the adventures of Annie and Popcorn. The days before school and tennis and legs too long to fit in Popcorn's tiny saddle.

"I wish I could have a new girl to play with," Popcorn thought to herself.

Popcorn wandered around her pasture, finding the most tender bites of grass. Then she dozed off under the shade of her favorite tree.

Loud noises woke Popcorn from her slumber. A big, noisy truck parked at the house behind Popcorn's pasture. Trees and bushes blocked most of the view, but there was a spot in the fence where Popcorn could check out what was going on. She watched people carrying boxes and furniture into the house. It looked like a new family was moving into the big house.

All day long, Popcorn watched as the people carried boxes into the house. With her children all grown up, Popcorn's daily life was a little boring, so she was happy to have something to amuse her for a while.

She must have drifted off to sleep again because she awoke with a start to the sound of small voices. Laughter and the sound of children's voices filled the air. Popcorn peeked back through the clearing in the hedge. A small girl and two boys were kicking a ball in the yard. Popcorn whinnied. The new family had kids!

The little girl stopped kicking the ball.

"Did you hear that?" she asked her brothers.

"Hear what?" one of them asked.

"It sounded like a pony," she said.

"I don't see any ponies," her brothers said.

Popcorn wanted to stick her head over the fence, but the hedge was too high and prickly. She could only whinny and hope the little girl would hear her.

It worked! Before too long, a little round face appeared in the clearing.

"I thought I heard a pony!" a little voice exclaimed.

The little girl stuck her hand through the clearing. Popcorn went over and rubbed her head against the girl's hand.

"Heehee, that tickles!" the girl giggled. "What's your name, pony? I wish you could tell me. I love ponies!"

Popcorn wished she could say, "My name is Popcorn, and I love kids!" But of course, she could only nicker to the girl.

"My name is Livvy. I'll come back to visit you later. Bye, pony!"

Livvy scurried down from the fence and hurried inside. Popcorn watched her go with a sense of excitement. Maybe Livvy would be Popcorn's new girl.

The next day, Popcorn ate her breakfast and went outside to nibble grass. She stayed close to the small clearing in the hedge so she could see if Livvy came back. Sure enough, around midday, her little face popped over the fence.

"Hi, pony!" she said. Popcorn walked over to the fence and nuzzled Livvy.

"I brought you a treat. I read that horses like carrots. Do you like carrots?" Livvy asked. She held out her hand to Popcorn and offered a piece of carrot. Popcorn loved carrots. She gently took the bite that Livvy offered and crunched it gratefully.

Livvy stayed for a long time. She told Popcorn all about their move. She missed her friends, but she was excited to make new ones. Livvy liked to dance, and her favorite color was purple. She loved all animals, but horses and dogs were her favorite.

The whole time she talked, she rubbed Popcorn's fur. She played with her mane. Popcorn snuggled Livvy's shoulder with her muzzle. Popcorn was delighted at all the attention.

Livvy came back several days in a row. Each time she came, she brought a little treat for Popcorn. Carrots, bits of apple, and sugar cubes were all some of Popcorn's favorite treats. Livvy also brought a hairbrush and spent time brushing Popcorn's silky mane. She even braided ribbons into her hair!

Popcorn spent most of her days now at the clearing near the fence. Annie even commented one morning, "You must have found some tasty grass over there. You never leave that spot anymore."

"That's where my new friend is," Popcorn thought.

One day, Livvy came to visit as she usually did. She brought a small cookie to share with Popcorn. She started braiding her mane, but she accidentally dropped her hairbrush into Popcorn's pasture.

"Oh no, pony! What am I going to do? I need to get that hairbrush back. But I'm not sure I'm allowed to come into your paddock. I know you won't hurt me, but I don't want to get in trouble."

Livvy sat and thought about it for a while. Popcorn wished she could pick the brush up and give it to Livvy. If only she had hands! Finally, Livvy said, "Maybe if I just climb the fence and get the hairbrush really quick and then climb back over. That way I won't get in trouble."

Popcorn was delighted with this plan. She had been secretly hoping Livvy would come to her side of the fence for a long time. She wished Livvy could stay longer. She wanted to go on adventures together. She wanted Livvy to ride her.

Livvy carefully climbed to the top of the fence. She put one foot over and started to climb down. Her shirt got caught on a prickly branch and made her lose her balance. Livvy fell off the fence and landed in Popcorn's pasture in a small heap on the ground.

Poor Livvy! She sat up quickly and hugged her legs to her body as the tears started. She was crying very hard. She had a scrape on her knee and a tear in her shirt. She looked so sad.

Popcorn did not know what to do. She nuzzled Livvy, but that didn't seem to make it better. Livvy was hurt. Popcorn knew she needed another human to help make her friend feel better.

Popcorn did the only thing she could think of to get attention. She ran around her pasture. She whinnied loudly. She ran to the gate closest to her house and whinnied. Then she ran around the pasture again. Popcorn was creating quite a commotion.

Finally, a door to the house opened. Annie came outside.

"Popcorn! What's wrong, sweet pony? Are you scared? Are you hurt?" Annie asked.

Popcorn whinnied and trotted over to the clearing in the fence where Livvy was still sitting and crying.

"Oh no! What's happened? Are you okay?" Annie asked Livvy.

Through her tears, Livvy answered, "I'm sorry. I was petting your pony and I dropped my brush. I fell trying to get it. I'm sorry. I didn't mean to be over here. I just love petting your pony."

"You've got a cut on your knee. I'm sure that hurts," Annie said. "I'm glad Popcorn came and got me to let me know you were here. Popcorn must really like you."

"The pony's name is Popcorn?" Livvy sniffled.

"Yep! And she loves kids. I'm glad you have been visiting Popcorn. That way she isn't lonely anymore," Annie reassured her. "I'll tell you what. Let's get you back home so you can get cleaned up. We can talk to your mom about letting you visit Popcorn more. Would you like that?"

"Oh yes!" Livvy sighed. "That would be a dream come true."

Annie helped Livvy stand up. She helped her get back to the other side of the fence. Then Annie climbed the fence, too, and walked Livvy home.

Popcorn waited at the fence to see what would happen. After some time, she saw Annie come back. Annie carefully climbed back into Popcorn's paddock. She gave Popcorn some good scratches under her mane and a kiss on her nose.

"Good job, sweet pony. Thank you for letting me know that the little girl was hurt."

The next morning, Popcorn didn't see Livvy. She worried about her friend. Maybe Livvy had gotten really hurt when she fell off the fence. Maybe Livvy's parents didn't want her to come see Popcorn anymore. Maybe they felt like ponies were too dangerous.

Around lunchtime, Annie came outside and put a halter on Popcorn. She led Popcorn into her stall and gave her a flake of hay.

"Sorry, girl," she said, "but we can't have you underfoot while we are working."

Annie closed the stall door and left Popcorn in the stall.

Popcorn could only see a little of what was happening out her window. She saw some tools and boards being carried to the little clearing in the fence. She heard lots of hammering and banging.

Popcorn started to worry. What if they were blocking the little clearing in the fence so Livvy couldn't visit her anymore? Maybe Livvy wasn't going to be allowed to see her ever again. This made Popcorn sad.

Finally, the banging stopped. The tools were put away. Annie came back into the barn and opened up Popcorn's door.

"Want to see what we have been doing?" she asked Popcorn.

She led Popcorn out of the barn and took off her halter so she could run around. Popcorn immediately decided to trot over to the little clearing and investigate.

Popcorn couldn't believe what she saw. There was a new gate installed in the little clearing. A new gate! This gate would make it so much easier for Livvy to come visit her.

Popcorn whinnied to Annie. When she turned back, Popcorn saw Livvy walking over to the gate.

"Hi, Livvy!" Annie said. "Are you ready for your first riding lesson?"

"Yes!" Livvy said proudly. "I'm even wearing new boots."

Livvy walked through the gate and exclaimed, "This gate makes seeing Popcorn so much easier!"

Annie laughed. "That's good because Popcorn hopes you will visit her every day. You can learn to ride her, and you guys will have so many adventures. My favorite memories are with Popcorn. I'm glad Popcorn has another little girl to love her."

Popcorn whinnied. She was glad. She loved Annie, and now she loved Livvy, too. She was excited for all the fun they were going to have together.

"Popcorn is the best pony ever!" Livvy exclaimed, and Annie agreed.

The New Girl

Riley had been riding since she was a baby. She loved horses. She even had her own horse! She lived two streets away from the barn where her horse lived. She could even ride her bike to go see him.

Riley's horse was named Spirit. He was a big, black horse with a white star on his forehead. Riley thought he looked like royalty. He had a long mane and tail that Riley loved to brush.

Riley went to the barn every day. She had lots of friends at the barn. Her best friend, Meg, also kept her horse at the barn. Meg's horse's name was Duke. Meg hadn't been riding as long as Riley, but she loved horses just as much.

Riley and Meg took lessons from Miss Donna. Riley had been riding with Miss

Donna for many years. She had learned a lot from her. Miss Donna had won a lot of horse shows. She took good care of her horses. Riley wanted to be just like her. She wanted to go to horse shows and win ribbons, too. Riley was one of Miss Donna's best students. She was one of the best riders at the stable.

When Riley got to the barn for her riding lesson, Miss Donna found her.

"I have a new student starting riding lessons today. She just moved here but has taken riding lessons before. Could you show her around and help her tack up Max?"

Riley was always happy to help Miss Donna. "Sure! I can help."

Riley brushed Spirit and got him ready. Then she noticed a new rider walk into the barn. Riley went and introduced herself.

"Hi! I'm Riley, and this is my horse, Spirit. Miss Donna asked me to show you around and help you tack up Max," she said.

"I'm Ella," the new rider said. "Thanks for helping me."

Riley showed Ella all around the barn. She showed her where they kept the brushes and all the saddles and bridles. She showed her where they groomed horses and where the arena was located. Last, she opened up Max's stall and introduced her to him.

"He is really pretty," Ella said. "He looks like a horse at my old barn."

"Do you need me to help you brush Max and tack him up?" Riley asked.

"I can do it, but thank you," Ella answered politely.

Riley hurried back to Spirit. She was ready to ride.

In the arena, Miss Donna introduced the class to Ella.

"Ella, what is your favorite thing about horses?" Miss Donna asked her.

"I love everything, but I really like to go to horse shows," Ella replied.

Some of the class started chattering right away. Going to a horse show sounded fun!

"Have you won any blue ribbons?" Meg asked.

"A few," said Ella.

"Wow!" said another girl. "You must be really good!"

Riley started to feel a little prickle of jealousy. She was used to being the best rider in the class. She wasn't sure she was going to like Ella.

The lesson started. Ella was a good rider. She fit right in with the class. She knew how to trot and canter. She jumped small jumps, just like Riley. Miss Donna still had to remind her to keep her hands quiet and keep her chin up.

"She's not THAT good," Riley thought to herself.

After the lesson, all the other girls crowded around Ella to ask about going to horse shows. They wanted to know what she wore, the name of the horse she rode, and what color ribbons she won.

"My favorite horse to ride was named Cloud Dancer. He had the smoothest canter. We almost always won first or second place," Ella told the girls. "But he was not a good jumper. For jumping, I liked to ride Lolly."

"I wish we could go to horse shows," said one girl dreamily.

Riley rolled her eyes. Miss Donna said that they still had things they needed to practice before they were ready for horse shows. She said horse shows were a lot of work. Riders needed to be prepared to handle their horses if the horse got nervous or excited. Sometimes going to horse shows made horses feel frisky. Miss Donna wanted her riders prepared.

Still, Riley couldn't help dreaming a little about being able to take Spirit to a horse show. He was so beautiful and such a good boy. She was sure he would win a blue ribbon. She wished she could show like Ella did.

Later the next week, several of the girls hurried to brush their horses after the lesson.

"Are you coming?" Meg asked Riley. "Ella is going to show us how to braid manes for a horse show."

Riley felt the prickle of jealousy again.

"No, I'm going to stay here and give Spirit an extra good brushing. He deserves it," Riley said.

"Suit yourself," Meg said. "I want to learn how to braid."

Riley spent a long time brushing Spirit. She combed his mane and tail until there were no more tangles. She used a soft brush until he was nice and shiny. She put hoof oil on his hooves. She thought about how fun it must be to go to a horse show.

She felt a little jealous that she and Spirit had never won any blue ribbons.

She was so involved in her work that she didn't hear Ella walk up with Max.

"Spirit looks so pretty," she told Riley.

"Thanks," Riley responded as she put the hoof oil lid back on the can. She put it in the cabinet and turned around. "Wow! That braid is really cool!"

"Thanks, it's not very good. I'm still learning, but it's fun to practice," Ella said.

"How did you do it?" Riley walked over and inspected the braid. It was like one long French braid that went down Max's mane.

"It's just like a French braid, except you only take one piece from the top. Like this...." She showed Riley at the end of Max's mane.

"Hmmmm, ok, I think I get it. I'm going to try it on Spirit," Riley told her.

"It helps to have a stool," Ella added. "I think it makes it easier to get the braid tight if I'm not reaching up so high."

"Oh, good idea!" Riley smiled as she grabbed a step stool.

She reached up and parted the mane into three pieces and began braiding.

"Like this?" she asked Ella, as she added little pieces of mane to the braid.

"Yep, really good!" Ella praised.

Riley concentrated hard as she worked her way down the mane. Ella gave little tips and encouraged her as she went. Finally, she got to the end of the mane. Ella handed her a black rubber band. Riley finished the braid, and they both stood back to admire the work.

"Wow, that's really good!" Ella said. "It looks so nice on Spirit."

"Thanks!" Riley grinned as she kissed Spirit's nose. "And thanks for showing me how to do it."

"Anytime. You are so lucky to have your own horse. I would give anything if my parents would let me get my own horse," Ella said wistfully.

Riley was quiet. She knew she was lucky to have Spirit. He was her best friend. Lately, she had been so busy being jealous of Ella that she forgot how lucky she was to have a horse of her very own. She wouldn't trade any amount of horse shows for the special bond she had with her horse.

"He's a good boy. He's my best friend," Riley said. "Do you think your parents will ever let you get a horse?"

Ella shrugged. "They always say, 'Maybe when you are older.' But it would be so fun to have a horse now. You get to ride whenever you want. And I'll bet you get to trail ride and ride bareback! Those are the best parts of riding."

Riley agreed. She loved riding Spirit around bareback, and she loved when she and Meg could go trail riding together.

Riley wasn't quite sure how to respond. She felt bad for Ella.

"I hope one day your parents let you get a horse of your own. You can ride Spirit bareback if you want," she told her.

"Really?!" Ella exclaimed. "That would be amazing! Thank you!"

"Yeah, of course! Why don't we try it next week after our lesson? That will be fun!" Riley was getting excited. She was happy to share her horse with her new friend.

"Thank you so much. Now I can't wait until next week," Ella laughed.

The two girls said goodbye, and Ella went out to meet her mom in the parking lot. Riley grabbed a few treats from the tack room. She gave Spirit treats and thought about how lucky she was to have him. She felt silly now for being jealous of Ella. Ella was right. Riding bareback, trail riding, and just being best friends with your horse were the best parts of riding horses anyway.

A Barn Mystery

Molly and Maggie finished their breakfast and put on their riding boots. They walked across the yard to the cozy two-stall barn where their ponies lived.

"Race ya!" Molly yelled as she took off running.

"No fair. You got a head start," Maggie complained.

The girls slowed just as they got to the barn door. They knew running in the barn wasn't a good idea. They didn't want to scare their ponies.

As they walked into the barn, Maggie noticed something.

"Did you leave that halter in the middle of the aisle?" she asked Molly.

"No, I always put my things away," Molly said, rolling her eyes. "Maybe you did!"

Maggie looked around thoughtfully as she picked up the halter and hung it on its hook across the barn. "No, I know the aisle was clear last night. Weird!"

The ponies began to whinny, demanding their breakfast.

"Okay, settle down! We're bringing your food!" Molly told them.

Molly and Maggie each had their own pony. Molly's pony was Jello. Maggie's pony was Kipper.

Molly and Maggie loved their ponies. They loved riding them and taking care of them.

Molly scooped the grain for the ponies, while Maggie got them hay and fresh water. As Maggie put the hose away, she noticed a bucket outside. It had been knocked over to its side. Maggie knew there had been a sponge in the bucket the day before.

She had used it to wash Kipper. Now that sponge was gone!

"Hey, Molly," she called to her sister. "Something weird is going on."

She told her about the bucket and the sponge. "Isn't it strange? And we had that halter in the middle of the aisle. I know we didn't leave it there."

Molly shrugged. "Who knows. Maybe it was a raccoon or one of the barn cats."

Since Molly didn't seem to be too concerned, Maggie tried not to be either. Maybe it really was a raccoon. Maggie decided to put it out of her mind. She had plenty of work to do.

The girls got to work cleaning stalls. They brushed their ponies and took them for a trail ride. On their ride, they noticed a new pony had moved in down the street. He looked up and whinnied as they rode past his paddock. The girls saw that the blackberries were starting to get ripe on the blackberry bushes. They stopped and picked a few for a quick snack. When they were done riding, they let the ponies out to graze in their field. The ponies rolled happily in the sunshine.

The missing sponge and the halter were forgotten. At least they were, until the next morning when the girls walked back into the barn.

"Okay, that's weird," Molly said as she reached down to pick up her halter. Both halters were lying in a pile in the middle of the barn aisle.

"First one halter and now both halters. It *is* weird, isn't it?" Maggie exclaimed.

The girls went about their morning routine, feeding the horses and getting them fresh water. When Molly went outside to get the wheelbarrow, she stopped suddenly. In the stable yard, the wheelbarrow had been knocked over.

Maggie hurried outside when her sister called her.

"That wheelbarrow was half full. It was heavy. This was definitely not the work of a raccoon! What do you think it is?" Maggie exclaimed.

Molly was starting to look a little nervous. "I don't know, but whatever it is, it seems to come around at night."

The girls looked around to see if anything else was out of place. They went inside and told their parents about the strange things that had been happening.

"It could be a raccoon," Dad said.

"Or maybe the wind. We did have a storm last night," Mom replied.

The girls went back to the barn. They sat together whispering in the tack room.

"This definitely isn't a raccoon," Maggie said.

"Or the wind," Molly added. "It feels mysterious. Do you think it could be a ghost?"

"A ghost?" Maggie asked, looking scared.

"Well, it seems to come around at night. It's too strong to be a raccoon or one of the barn cats. Plus, that sponge was just gone! Like it vanished," Molly said.

The more Maggie and Molly thought about it, the more they thought that it might be a ghost.

"Do you think it's a mean ghost? Does it not like ponies?" Maggie asked.

"I don't know, but we need to make sure our ponies are safe. Maybe we should set a trap."

Maggie didn't know if you could trap a ghost, but it couldn't hurt to try. The girls spent the rest of the day working on a ghost trap.

"Even if it doesn't trap the ghost, it will keep our ponies safe," Molly told her sister. The girls had used lunge lines and rope to weave a web at both ends of the cozy barn, blocking anything from getting in or out. By the time they were finished, they were too tired to ride.

"We will definitely ride tomorrow," Molly told Jello as she kissed her goodnight.

Early the next morning, Maggie gently shook Molly awake. "Wake up," she whispered. "We need to go check our trap."

Molly hurried out of bed, and the two girls ran across the yard in their pajamas. Molly wasn't sure what they would find. She was a little nervous. What if they really did trap a ghost? What if the ghost was mad?

When they got to the barn, Molly was slightly relieved to see that they had not caught a ghost. Something had definitely been there, though. And whatever it was had caused a lot of trouble. The pony blankets that usually sat just outside their stalls had been pulled out of the barn. Jello's blanket was all the way out in the yard! One of the lawn chairs in the yard had been tipped on its side. On the other end of the barn, even an entire horse jump had been knocked over.

"Do you think we made it mad?" Maggie wondered.

The girls cleaned up the mess and got to work with their morning chores. They had promised their ponies a fun ride. Even though they were nervous about the ghost, they got out their saddles anyway.

The ride turned out to be a good idea. It was good to relieve some stress. They cantered along the dusty trail, ate blackberries, and waved at the new pony down the road. They were tired and full of smiles when they rode back into their own yard later in the day.

That night, the girls told their parents about the ghost, their ghost trap, and the mess that had been made in the stable yard. This time, their parents looked a bit more concerned.

"Hmmm... that doesn't sound like something a raccoon could do. It is a little concerning. We will stay up tonight and keep an eye on things," Dad told them.

"Can we sleep in the barn?" Molly asked.

"A barn sleepover! PLEEEEASE!" Maggie begged.

"Okay, we can put some cots in the tack room," Dad replied.

The girls excitedly gathered all the things they would need for a barn sleepover. Cots, sleeping bags, pillows, and stuffed animals all made the trip to the barn. Molly packed some late-night snacks and even a bag of carrots for the ponies.

"Now we are ready!" Maggie exclaimed.

With their parents with them, Molly and Maggie were not nearly as nervous about the ghost. Their parents kept telling them that it wasn't a ghost. But what else could it be?

They stayed up late, eating snacks and giggling. They even watched a movie on Mom's computer. Soon it was late, and time to get some rest. The girls went out to the stalls and kissed their ponies goodnight. Then they climbed into their cots and fell asleep in no time at all.

Maggie heard the noise first. She had been dreaming about cats when a soft thumping woke her up.

Thump, thump, thump.

Maggie sat up in bed.

Thump, thump, thump.

The noise was getting louder.

"Dad! Something's out there!" she whispered loudly.

Dad sat up groggily. Then he heard the noise, too.

Molly and Maggie stood up. They followed their dad to the door. He pulled it open quietly and shined a flashlight out into the barn aisle.

There, in the middle of the barn aisle, was another pony. Not Jello or Kipper, but a third pony!

"Hey, that's the new pony from down the road!" Maggie exclaimed.

"You're right!" Molly said. "Do you think he is the one that has been causing all these messes?"

Mom walked out into the aisle, and the friendly pony walked over to her.

"I'll bet this is your ghost," Mom laughed. "He could easily pull halters and blankets off the stall doors, knock over jumps and wheelbarrows, and even run off with your sponge!"

The girls giggled and went to meet the new pony. He seemed to already be good friends with Kipper and Jello. The thumping noise they had heard was Jello, banging her hoof against the stall door to try and get her new friend's attention. The new pony had already pulled the halters off the hooks and tipped over a bucket of brushes.

"It seems like he's the culprit!" Dad said as he put things back in their place. The girls found an old halter in the tack room to use on the visitor. They put him securely in the small paddock behind the barn where he would be safe until they could take him back to his proper home in the morning.

The next morning, the girls and their parents led the pony down the road back to his home. As they were walking up the driveway, a young girl came running out of the house.

"Mischief! Mischief! Oh, where have you been? You naughty pony! I have been so worried about you!"

"He's been down the road, visiting our ponies," Molly told her. "I'm Molly and this is my sister, Maggie. Your pony has been visiting our ponies every night for the past couple of days."

The girl nodded her head. "That makes sense. Poor Mischief. We only moved here last week. I think he is lonely. My name is Hannah."

"Your pony's name is Mischief?" Molly asked. "That's funny because he has certainly been causing mischief at our barn."

"We thought he was a ghost!" Maggie added.

"Oh, I hope he didn't cause too much trouble," Hannah worried.

"No, not at all. It was just funny. He does like to get into things, doesn't he?"

"His name is Mischief because he is good at escaping and always getting into trouble," Hannah told them, smiling.

"If you and Mischief need friends, we go riding almost every day. You should join us!" Molly said.

"That sounds amazing! Can I?" Hannah asked, looking at her parents.

"Yes, of course, but how about breakfast first?" her mom said.

The girls made plans to meet later in the day, and Molly, Maggie, and their parents walked back to their house.

"I'm glad our barn isn't haunted," Molly said.

"And I'm glad a silly pony named Mischief introduced us to a new friend," Maggie added.

The Pony Wish

Ava had dreamed of having a pony of her own for as long as she could remember. She asked for a pony of her own for her birthday every year. So far, all she had gotten were horse stuffed animals and toys. Those were fun, but not as fun as a real pony. One year she even had a horse-themed birthday party, hoping her parents would consider a horse as part of the deal. It hadn't worked. She had pony napkins, pony plates, and a pretty pony cake, but no actual pony showed up for her.

Her birthday was in two weeks, but Ava had given up on getting a pony for her birthday. She was going to visit her grandparents soon. She always loved spending time with them. She and her grandma would bake cookies. Grandpa would teach her games and read stories.

The best part was the pony that lived just up the street. While she was there, Ava could go visit the pony every day. She would bring him carrots and apples and pretend that he was her pony. She never saw anybody riding or even spending time with the pony, so it was easy to pretend that he was hers.

When Ava arrived at her grandparents' house, she started unpacking her suitcase. She brought her favorite pair of boots so she could pretend she was going to ride the pony. Grandma showed her some new books she had gotten Ava. One was even about a horse! Ava couldn't wait to read it, but first, it was time to eat lunch.

Ava's grandma made them chicken salad sandwiches while her grandpa poured them lemonade.

"What do you want to do this week, Ava?" her grandpa asked.

"Well, you told me I could help you in your shop. I want to learn how to build things," she said. Her grandpa liked to build things out of wood. Ava liked watching him measure and cut the wood, then nail it together to make new things.

Grandpa chuckled. "You do, huh? Well, I'm sure we can come up with something special to build. In the meantime, would you like to go for a walk?"

Ava nodded. She put on her boots, getting excited to see the neighbor's pony. She grabbed a few carrots before they headed out the door.

The air was cool with a chilly wind. Colorful leaves were falling off the trees and swirling in the wind. Ava grabbed a pretty red one and showed her grandpa. As they got close to the neighbor pony, Ava started looking for him over the fence. Usually, she could spot him quickly. He would see them coming and walk over to the fence to greet them.

This time he wasn't as easy to spot. Instead of coming to see them, he stayed in the far corner, with his head hanging down. He looked tired and sad.

"Here, boy!" Ava called. She clucked to encourage him.

The pony raised his head a little and gave a deep sigh. Ava clucked to him, and he finally began to walk their way.

As he got closer, Ava couldn't believe her eyes. The pony looked pitiful. He had gotten very skinny and had big knots in his mane.

"He's not looking so good," Grandpa said. "Do you think he is sick?"

"Maybe. He doesn't look like he is eating. He's so skinny," Ava whispered in disbelief.

The pony was finally close enough for them to touch. His eyes seemed sad, and his nose was runny. His ribs were showing, and he didn't want to lift his head high. He looked tired. His coat, once shiny and soft, was now dull and dirty. His mane and tail had big knots, and his hooves had cracks.

"Ava, do you see any hay or anything for this pony to eat?" Grandpa asked.

Ava looked around. She didn't see any hay and hardly any grass that might feed the pony. She finally saw a trough next to the fence on the other side. She went over and checked to see if it had anything in it. Her heart sank when she realized that the trough only held a few inches of very dirty water. Not only did this poor pony not have any food, he didn't even have clean water. A little shed that had once offered shelter from the rain looked like it had fallen down in a storm.

Ava was getting angry. This poor pony was locked in this pasture with no food, water, or shelter. He looked sick and sad. Where were the owners of this pony?

Ava could tell her grandpa was worried about the pony, too. He looked around to see if there was a house near the pasture, but there were just woods on either side. It was almost like the pony was all alone. Grandpa called a friend who lived nearby. He didn't know anything either, but he said he would ask around. While Grandpa was on the phone, Ava searched around the fence line. She found a water spigot and hose. She turned on the water and cleaned out the water trough. Then she filled it with fresh water. Ava didn't care if she got in trouble for messing with someone else's pony. The owners didn't seem to care about him. The poor pony drank the fresh water gratefully.

"Well, Ava, we need to head back to the house. There isn't anything we can do for this pony right now. I'll make some phone calls and see if we can figure out who he belongs to," Grandpa told her.

"Who cares who he belongs to! They aren't taking good care of him," Ava protested. "Can't we keep him?"

"We can't just take a pony. Besides, where would we keep him? Come on, let's go home, and I can work on a solution."

Ava felt like she didn't have a choice, so she gave the pony one last good scratch and followed Grandpa home.

At home, Grandpa explained the situation to Grandma. Grandma loved animals, so Ava knew she would help them, too. Grandpa made some phone calls. He finally learned that the pony belonged to a man named Mr. Adams. He lived about a mile away. Grandpa tried to call him, but no one answered the phone.

"We should go over to his house," Ava declared. "He needs to take care of his pony."

Grandma looked thoughtful as she watched the weather. A worried expression crept onto her face. "We really don't have much time. There is a big storm coming tomorrow. There will be lots of wind and cold rain. We need to figure out how to help the pony before the storm hits."

With that news, it was decided. They got in the car and drove to Mr. Adams' house. The house didn't look any better than the horse pasture. The yard was overgrown, and a shutter hung loose.

Ava stayed in the car while Grandpa went to talk to Mr. Adams. She watched closely to see if Mr. Adams looked concerned. He never did. Ava thought he looked grouchy. Finally, Grandpa walked back to the car. He got in and sighed.

"Mr. Adams isn't going to do anything to help the pony. He said he doesn't want him anymore, and he's tired of feeding him."

"Tired of feeding him?!" Ava exclaimed. "He should go to jail for that!"

"Well, I don't know what the laws are, but Mr. Adams did say we could help the pony. So I guess that's what we'll do," Grandpa said. "We can at least go to the farm store and get him some hay."

"Oh, thank you, Grandpa!" Ava yelped as she threw her arms around her grandpa.

After a quick trip to the farm store to get some hay and basic supplies, Ava and her grandparents drove back to the pony's pasture. The pony immediately started to gobble up the hay when Ava threw it over the fence. Ava spent some time patting and loving on the pony while he ate. After a while, a truck pulled up.

"Who's this?" Ava asked worriedly.

"This is a friend of mine," said Grandma. "She is a vet, and she is going to take a look at the pony and see if he is sick."

"Hi, I'm Dr. Carter," the lady said. "You've done a good job taking care of this pony. Can I take a look?"

After a quick exam, Dr. Carter explained that the pony wasn't sick, just very skinny. He would need lots of love and care to gain weight and feel well again. Ava brushed the knots in the pony's mane while the adults talked. She started to notice that they were looking worried again. They talked in hushed voices so she couldn't hear what they were saying.

Finally, Grandpa came over. "Ava, remember how you wanted to learn how to build things with me in my shop?"

"Yep," Ava said, looking puzzled.

"Well, I think we've got ourselves a special project. Dr. Carter thinks the pony will get sick if he is left outside during the storm tomorrow night. It is supposed to be really wet and cold. I've got some extra room in my woodshop. Do you think you could help me build this little guy a stall to keep him safe from the storm? We can build the stall and walk him over to the house. That way, you can feed him and take care of him. Dr. Carter says it will be a lot of work to get this guy feeling better. Are you up for the task?"

"Oh, yes! Of course! This pony can count on me to take care of him," Ava grinned.

"Well, we'd better get to work!"

Back at home, Grandpa came up with a plan. The corner of his shop didn't have anything in it, and it would be a safe, dry place for the pony. Grandpa got to work. He showed Ava how to measure the wood he needed. Grandpa used his saw to cut the wood, then he and Ava worked together to nail it into place.

Measure. Cut. Nail. Measure. Cut. Nail. The little stall started to take shape.

Grandma brought their dinner to them out in the shop. She was impressed with their work. As they sat around and ate dinner, they talked about the pony.

“What are we going to call him?” Grandma asked.

Ava thought hard about it. She had been thinking of it while she worked building the stall. She knew she probably wouldn’t get to keep the pony. Her family lived in the city, and there was no room for a pony. Still, she was happy to play a role in helping him feel better.

“I need some more time to think about it,” Ava said. She knew the perfect name would come along.

Later that night, as she was getting ready for bed, Ava sat and looked out the window. The stall was close to being done. She and Grandpa needed to finish it in the morning. She would put down some soft bedding in the stall, hang a bucket of fresh water, and put in plenty of hay. Then it would be ready for a pony.

Ava made a wish as she looked at the stars. She wished that the pony would come to the little stall they built and start to feel better. She wished that he would feel loved and special again. And she wished that his future would be better than his past. She made an extra secret wish that she would be able to keep him for herself. Then Ava crawled under the covers and fell fast asleep.

The next day, Ava and Grandpa finished their project. They cheered when the stall was all done and ready for the pony. Grandma came in and admired their work.

"Just in time, too," she told them. "The storm will be here soon."

The three of them walked to the pony's paddock. Ava found a halter and slipped it on his head. The pony looked surprised when Grandma opened the gate and Ava tried to lead him out of his paddock.

"I promise you'll like it," she told him. "It's way better than here."

The pony timidly followed her out of the gate. She slipped him a carrot as they started the walk home. The pony seemed to grow more excited with each step. He snorted happily and rubbed his head against Ava. She giggled and stroked his neck.

Ava held her breath when she led the pony into his stall. She really wanted him to like it. The pony turned around slowly, sniffing everything. He took a sip of water and nibbled the hay. Finally, he laid down and rolled in the fresh bedding. He groaned happily as he stood back up and walked over to Ava. He seemed to be telling her that he liked his new stall.

About that time, the rain started. It was a cold rain, with lots of wind. Grandma brought their sandwiches out to the barn so they could eat lunch with their new friend.

"Have you figured out what you are going to call him?" Grandpa asked.

Ava thought about the night before, looking at the stars and making a wish for the pony to be happy again—a wish that was full of hope and promise.

"I think I want to call him Wish," Ava told her grandparents.

Grandma nodded. "That's a good name. It seems hopeful."

Ava smiled. That's exactly what she was going for by naming him Wish.

Ava spent all day out in the barn with Wish. She brushed him, fed him treats, and even read books to him. Wish seemed to enjoy her company. And he definitely liked his cozy new stall, especially as the storm continued outside. The stall was dry and warm, with soft bedding and yummy things to nibble. It seemed to Ava that Wish was already much happier.

As Ava and her grandparents tucked Wish into his stall for the night, Ava finally asked the question she had been pondering. "What will we do with Wish when he is all better?"

Grandma looked thoughtful. "Well, we have a granddaughter who just loves ponies. She asks for one every year for her birthday. She has a birthday coming up, so I suppose we will just give him to her for her birthday."

Ava's eyes widened. "Really? I get to keep Wish? He's going to be mine?"

Grandpa laughed. "We are still working out all the details, but yes, we built this nice stall. I'd hate for it to go to waste."

Ava threw her arms around Wish, then hugged her grandparents. "My birthday wish finally came true!"

Never Give Up

"I have some exciting news!" Miss Finch announced to the group of riding students gathered around. "We are going to host a Games Day for the horse club in three weeks. We will have barrel racing, pole bending, relay races, and other fun games for horses and riders. We will spend the next few weeks learning all of these games and practicing them with our horses. Then we will have a little friendly competition!"

The group of riding students talked excitedly. The chance to learn and play new games with their horses, along with an opportunity to compete, sounded like a lot of fun.

Lucy ran a hand over her horse, Scout. The bay gelding was fast. Lucy knew she would have a good shot at winning some of the games. She grinned to herself as she thought about it.

Lucy was part of a horse club called Hoofprints. Miss Finch was their leader and helped them learn all about horses. She taught them about horse care. They learned about the best things to feed their horses. They learned about vet care and hoof care. Best of all, Lucy got to hang out with other horse-loving friends and spend time doing nothing but horse-related activities!

Lucy was horse-crazy. She had owned Scout for one year. She loved riding and taking care of him. Scout was fast and sometimes stubborn, but he was also sweet. He loved and trusted Lucy.

"Are you guys ready to learn some of the games?" Miss Finch asked.

"Yeah!" The group cheered.

Miss Finch told them about barrel racing. There were three barrels set up in a triangular pattern. The top barrel was the furthest away. The horse and rider would run in and choose either the left or right barrel. They would run around it, then proceed to the next barrel and run around that one. Finally, they would run to the top barrel, circle around it, and then race all the way back to the gate. The event was timed. The fastest time would win first place.

"That sounds easy enough," Lucy told her best friend, Haley.

"Maybe," Haley said with a bit of nervousness in her voice. Haley didn't really like to go fast.

Miss Finch set up the barrel pattern, and the kids started to take turns.

"It's not about speed at this point. It's more important to get your horse used to the barrels and the pattern."

"My horse just wants to go fast!" Cole said as his horse zoomed up to the barrels.

When it was Lucy's turn, she asked Scout to trot. Scout entered the arena at a fast trot, but when he saw the barrel, he shied away from it. Scout didn't want to go anywhere near the barrels!

Miss Finch had Lucy slow down to a walk. Scout was still scared of the barrels. Lucy had to get off of Scout and walk him over to the barrel. Scout snorted at the barrel. Lucy sighed. This was going to take a lot of work if she wanted to do well on Games Day.

For the next few days, Lucy practiced with Scout. She was patient and tried to teach him that the barrels weren't scary. First, she practiced leading him around the barrels. Once he learned how to do that, she got on and walked him around the barrels. By the end of the week, Lucy could trot Scout around the barrels. Finally, Scout wasn't scared of the barrels.

At the next horse club meeting, Lucy was excited to show Miss Finch everything she had been practicing. She watched some of the other kids ride their horses through the barrel pattern. Wow! Some of them were really fast. Lucy started to get a little nervous. She wasn't sure she could go that fast yet on Scout. She sat waiting her turn, trying not to get too nervous. Haley was up next on her horse. Lucy watched Haley trot her horse into the arena. Haley's horse wasn't fast, but she did a quick turn around the barrels. She made up a lot of time with her quick turns.

"Great job, Haley!" Miss Finch told her. "Even if you don't like to go fast, you can still do well if you can train your horse to make tight turns."

Haley grinned. Lucy felt a little better. If she couldn't go fast, maybe she and Scout could still make tight turns.

Lucy was up next. She asked Scout to trot. This time, Scout was ready. He was feeling brave. He trotted boldly into the arena... and trotted right past the first barrel! Lucy was trying to turn him, but he wasn't listening. She finally managed to get him to make a huge turn around the first barrel. The second and third barrels weren't any better. Lucy's time was one of the slowest yet.

Lucy was feeling discouraged. No one else seemed to be having as much trouble with this as she was. She and Scout weren't very good. Lucy wasn't sure she wanted to barrel race anymore. Maybe she didn't want to ride Scout on Games Day.

Miss Finch came over to her. She seemed to know that Lucy was feeling down.

"I had a lot of trouble with my first horse, Pepper, when I taught him barrel racing. Pepper wanted to run past the barrels. He didn't like to turn. When I finally did get him turning, sometimes he would go around the barrels twice! It took me forever to finally teach him what he needed to do."

"How did you do it?" Lucy asked.

"Lots of hard work. I didn't give up. We kept working, and every time we practiced, we got a little bit better. That's the key. Just work a little bit every day. You will start to see improvements," Miss Finch encouraged.

Lucy nodded slowly. It made sense, but she still wasn't sure it would work for her and Scout. "Did he finally get better? Was Pepper ever good at barrel racing?" she asked.

Miss Finch pointed to her shiny silver belt buckle. "He sure did! Pepper won this belt buckle and four others. He was an awesome barrel-racing horse! He just needed me to take my time and train him slowly. Scout will figure it out. He is smart, and he loves you."

Lucy kept working on her barrel racing. She tried to get just a little bit better every day. Some days were easier than others. Scout still wanted to run past the barrels. He was not good at making tight turns.

After one bad day of practice, Lucy told her mom, "I don't think I like this. I think I'm going to quit."

"Learning new things can take time. It can be frustrating. It's important to keep trying. Won't you be sad if you don't get to participate in Game Day?" her mom said.

"I guess," Lucy grumbled. She decided to keep practicing, but she still kind of wanted to quit.

Then, slowly, Lucy and Scout started to get better. Scout was finally used to the barrels, but now he had to learn to turn. Lucy had never ridden in a barrel race before, so she was learning right along with Scout. She began to feel proud of her work. The very first time she got Scout to make a tight turn, Lucy whooped with excitement!

"Yeah, Scout! Good job, buddy!"

Each day, she aimed to get just a little bit better. And each day, Scout improved just a little bit. Lucy even began to ask Scout to canter up to the barrels. He listened to her, slowed down, and made the turn. Then she would ask him to canter to the next barrel. It was fun being so in sync with her horse.

On Game Day, Lucy woke up feeling excited and a little nervous. She hoped all of her hard work would show when she rode Scout. She saddled him up and rode him over to Miss Finch's arena. All of her friends were there. Everyone chattered excitedly about all the games.

They started the day with a relay race. Haley and Lucy were partners. Their horses were friends, just like the girls. They were good at the relay race and even won a red ribbon!

The next event was the Egg and Spoon race. The rider had to carry an egg on a spoon while riding their horse. The announcer would ask the riders to walk, trot, and canter. The last rider with an egg still on the spoon was declared the winner. Lucy laughed and laughed. Scout had a very bouncy trot. She was doing well until they had to do a sitting trot. Then her egg flopped to the ground. Oh well, it was still a fun game.

Finally, it was time to barrel race. Lucy had been training for this moment for weeks. She watched all of her friends and cheered for them. When it was her turn, she took a deep breath. She just wanted to go out there and show them everything she had been working on.

"You've got nothing to lose! Just give it your best shot!" her mom cheered.

Lucy walked up to the arena. She asked Scout to pick up a canter. Scout cantered up to the first barrel and made a tight turn.

"YESSS!!!!" Lucy cheered. She guided Scout to the next barrel. He gathered himself and did another awesome turn.

"One more!" Lucy told him as they headed to the final barrel. Once more, Scout cantered up to the barrel and glided around it smoothly.

"Whooo!!! Go!!!" Lucy whooped as she let Scout fly back to the gate. She pulled him to a stop at the end of the arena, grinning from ear to ear.

Lucy reached down and stroked Scout's neck. He was prancing with excitement. Scout looked just as proud as Lucy.

"Good boy!" she told him.

"Wow, that was a great run! Scout is fast," Cole told her. "I've never seen him run that fast before."

"I think Scout likes barrel racing," Lucy said, smiling. "We both do!"

Lucy watched the rest of her friends finish their barrel racing patterns. It was fun to cheer and holler for everyone. When the whole group was done, Miss Finch gave out the awards. Lucy was so happy when Miss Finch attached a yellow ribbon to Scout's bridle.

"Wow! Third place!" Lucy's mom cheered. "Scout is doing so well."

"I'm so proud of him. I'm proud of myself, too. I'm glad I didn't quit," Lucy told her mom.

Miss Finch came over to congratulate her. "Scout looks like a different horse than at his last practice. How did you do it?"

"We did just what you said and tried to get just a little bit better every day," Lucy told her. "Sometimes I wanted to quit, but I'm so glad I kept trying."

"It's important not to give up. Just try to get a little better every day. I think you and Scout will be winning lots of ribbons and buckles in the future!" Miss Finch told her.

Lucy gave Scout a big hug. She was glad she had kept working, even when things were tough. She loved Scout, and now she loved barrel racing, too.

Homesick

Ruby was so excited that she couldn't sleep. Tomorrow, she was going to her first overnight camp. She was going to take her pony, Delilah, to Stoney River Camp. They were going to spend five incredible days and nights together with other horse-crazy kids. Stoney River offered trail riding, jumping, swimming with ponies, and on the last night, a "sleep under the stars" trail ride and sleepover. Ruby had read the camp brochure so many times she practically had it memorized. It was going to be the highlight of her summer.

Ruby's best friend, Piper, and her pony, George, were coming, too. George and Delilah were best friends, just like Ruby and Piper. They were going to have stalls next to each other at camp. Ruby and Piper were going to share bunk beds.

Ruby tossed and turned, trying to fall asleep. Finally, she gave up and tiptoed downstairs. Her mom and dad were sitting in the living room watching a movie.

"Hey, Kiddo!" her dad said. "What's going on?"

"I'm too excited to sleep," Ruby answered.

Her mom and dad let her sit with them for a little while. Then Ruby's mom led her into the kitchen. She got her a glass of water and gave her a hug. She walked Ruby to her bedroom and tucked her into bed.

After one more hug, Ruby asked, "Could you stay for a minute?"

Ruby's mom nodded. She sat down beside Ruby and rubbed her back. It didn't take Ruby long to fall asleep after that.

The next morning was a flurry of activity. Ruby's dad got the horse trailer ready while Ruby and her mom did a last-minute check on all of her gear.

"Suitcase, sleeping bag, pillow?" her mom asked.

"Yep, got it all!" Ruby replied.

"Saddle, bridle, tack trunk, and Delilah's hay?"

"Got all that, too! We sure have to bring a lot when we take a pony to camp with us!" Ruby laughed.

When everything was checked off the list, all that was left to do was load Delilah into the trailer and drive to camp.

"Piper and George will be there later tonight," Ruby's mom told her. "They have to stop on the way and visit Piper's grandma. They won't be late, though."

And they were off! Ruby sat in the back seat dreaming of galloping Delilah through fields and splashing Piper in the river. Three hours later, her family's truck and horse trailer were pulling into the gates of Stoney River Camp!

The first job was to get Delilah settled at the horse barn. Ruby carefully unloaded her from the trailer while her mom filled her water bucket and her dad got Delilah a flake of hay. Delilah walked into her new stall and sniffed around. She went over to the side to see if she had a neighbor but found the stall next door empty.

"Don't worry. George will be here soon," Ruby told her.

Ruby unloaded all of her tack and made sure Delilah was well taken care of. Then they took Ruby's things to her cabin. Ruby and Piper were sharing a bunk bed in the "Topaz" cabin. Piper had a bunk bed at home, so she didn't mind if Ruby got to sleep on the top bunk. Ruby's mom and dad helped her unpack her things and make her bed. They explored around the camp and ate lunch together. Then it was time for her parents to go.

Ruby felt a little lump in her throat as she got ready to say goodbye. She was so excited about camp, but she was going to miss her parents.

Ruby's mom unzipped a side pocket on Ruby's suitcase.

"I know you are a big girl now, and you are old enough to go to overnight camp. But just in case you get a little lonely or homesick, I packed your favorite old blanket in here if you need it. I gave it a big hug before I packed it, so you can hug it and pretend you are hugging me," Ruby's mom told her. "You will have a wonderful time, and we can't wait to pick you up and hear all about it."

"Take good care of Delilah and go on lots of adventures," her dad added.

Ruby waved to her parents as their car disappeared down the driveway. She headed over to the barn to wait for Piper. While she waited, Ruby met other campers and their horses. Some of the campers had their own horses. Others were using horses that belonged to the camp.

Finally, Ruby saw Piper walk into the barn.

"I felt like you would never get here! Where is George?" Ruby asked. She looked at Piper and realized her friend had been crying.

"He's not coming. Well, he's not coming today. We had a problem with our trailer. My dad has to fix it, then he will bring George. It may take a few days. I can ride one of the camp horses, but it's not the same as George." Piper's lip trembled as she told this to Ruby.

Ruby felt horrible for her friend. She knew she would be sad if she didn't have Delilah with her. She tried to cheer her up.

"I'm so sorry. Hopefully George will be here very soon. You can learn something new with every horse you ride. I'm sure you will get along great with any horse you get. And I hear they are having ice cream sundaes for dessert tonight!" Ruby linked her arm through Piper's. Piper grinned, and the two went out to meet her parents and unload her suitcase into the "Topaz" cabin.

The girls had a wonderful first evening of camp. They met the rest of the girls in the "Topaz" cabin. They ate spaghetti for dinner and followed it with ice cream sundaes and extra sprinkles. Then they went for a late-night bareback ride around the arena with the rest of their group. Piper rode a horse named Butterscotch. She was really sweet and made Piper feel better.

Everyone headed back to the cabins for lights out. Ruby put on her pajamas and brushed her teeth. She climbed onto the top bunk and tried to fall asleep. She really tried, but she just couldn't. This bed wasn't the same as her bed at home. The noises in the cabin weren't the same as the noises in her room. She missed her little nightlight that kept the room from being too dark.

The crickets chirped gently outside. Ruby thought about what her mom and dad were doing at home. Maybe they were watching a movie. Or maybe they were sitting in bed reading books. Ruby remembered the night before when she had sat up with them when she couldn't sleep. She wished she could go see them right now. Her mom would know just what to say to help her fall asleep.

Ruby felt a tear slide down her cheek. She was feeling homesick. She had been so excited about all the adventures she would have at camp that she hadn't even thought about how much she would miss her parents. Another tear trickled onto her pillow. She wished she could just go home. Ruby thought about waking up their cabin counselor. Maybe she could call her parents, and they could come get her. But Ruby remembered how far away the camp was from her house. And it was the middle of the night.

Ruby lay in bed for a long time, feeling sad. Then she remembered something! She remembered the blanket her mom had tucked into the side pocket of her suitcase, the blanket with the giant mom hug! Ruby climbed down the ladder as quietly as she could. She unzipped the pocket and pulled out the blanket. The soft pink blanket had been her favorite when she was a little girl. It slept in her bed every night. She took it everywhere. She felt relieved when she touched the soft blanket. Ruby pressed the blanket to her face. It smelled like home. Ruby climbed back up to the top bunk. She hugged the blanket tightly and pretended she was hugging her mom and dad. Finally, Ruby was able to fall asleep.

Ruby felt much better the next morning. Knowing that she had the blanket felt like she had a little piece of home with her. She was ready to start the adventures of the day.

After breakfast, the girls ran to the barn. Ruby and Piper had to do their horse chores before they could do any riding. They fed the horses and cleaned their stalls. Then it was time to give the horses a good brushing. Ruby brushed Delilah's mane until it was silky and smooth. She picked her feet to make sure there were no pebbles or stones in them. Finally, it was time to ride!

The first ride was a lesson. Ruby was excited to see that jumps were set up. She and Delilah were just learning to jump at home. She wanted a chance to practice more.

Miss Kari, the instructor, showed Ruby a few new things to try. Ruby sat up a little taller. She kept her eyes focused over the jump, instead of looking straight at it. Miss Kari told her this would help Delilah know where to go. Ruby gave it a try. It worked! Delilah jumped the crossrail and cantered away proudly.

"Great job!" Miss Kari praised. Ruby beamed.

The rest of the lesson was fun. They did some jumping and played some horse games. At the end, they pulled off their saddles and cooled their ponies out by riding bareback.

"Camp is the best," Ruby sighed as she slid down off of Delilah.

Ruby and Piper brushed the ponies and found their assigned paddocks for turnout. Ruby knew Delilah would be so happy to go outside and munch on some grass. Butterscotch was turned out with some of the other camp horses. Delilah was assigned to go outside with George. Ruby knew it was best for the horses to go out in small groups, especially if they didn't know each other. It would help prevent fighting and possibly having a horse get hurt.

"I'm sorry, Delilah," Ruby told her. "I hope George will be here soon so you don't have to be alone."

Delilah walked around her new paddock. She sniffed the grass. She looked for a friend but couldn't find one. She whinnied to the horses in the next pasture over, but they were busy eating grass. Ruby hoped Delilah would feel better soon.

The afternoon was a busy one. Ruby and Piper learned how to canoe. They made picture frames out of horseshoes. They learned to put fancy braids in their horses' manes. They even went for a quick sunset trail ride after dinner. They topped off the evening singing songs around the campfire.

"It was a great first day of camp, but I hope George gets here soon," Piper told Ruby.

Ruby put her arm around her friend. "Me too!"

As they got ready for bed, Ruby started to get a little bit nervous. Would she be able to sleep? Would she get homesick tonight? She pulled the blanket tight as she got into bed. She smelled its soft scent that reminded her of home and thought of her parents. She couldn't wait to tell them all about camp. Ruby drifted peacefully to sleep.

The next morning, Ruby and Piper were ready for another day of camp adventures. That afternoon, they were going on a big trail ride down to the lake. At the lake, they would get to take their horses swimming! Ruby had never been swimming with Delilah, and she couldn't wait.

When she got to the barn to feed Delilah, something didn't seem right. Delilah stayed in the back of her stall. She didn't come over to see Ruby. She looked depressed.

"Hi, girl! Ready for your breakfast?" Ruby asked. Delilah sniffed her food and took a small bite. Then she sighed and walked away.

"Miss Kari! Something is wrong with Delilah!" Ruby shouted.

Miss Kari came over. Ruby explained what was going on. Miss Kari checked Delilah. She took her temperature and listened to her belly. She checked around her stall.

"Well, she doesn't have a fever. Her belly sounds good. She ate and drank last night and pooped. You were right to come get me. Delilah doesn't seem like herself. Let's keep a close eye on her. If she doesn't perk up soon, we may have to call the vet, and you can ride a different horse later," Miss Kari told her.

Ruby nodded, feeling scared. She didn't want anything to be wrong with her pony. Delilah was her best friend.

"Poor pony," Ruby said, hugging her horse. Delilah slowly nibbled at her grain, but she seemed to be sad. Ruby hoped she wasn't getting sick.

The other campers went to arts and crafts, but Ruby and Piper asked if they could stay with Delilah. They brushed her and tried to make her feel better. It was no use. Delilah just seemed sad.

Later in the morning, as they were sitting outside of Delilah's stall, they heard a truck pull up. A horse outside whinnied. Delilah whinnied back frantically.

"Who could that be?" Ruby asked.

The girls walked outside.

"Dad! George!" Piper called with excitement.

"Hey there! Sorry I couldn't tell you I was coming. I got the trailer fixed as soon as I could. I knew you would want to have George here with you. Should we get him off the trailer?" Piper's dad said as Piper gave him a big hug.

On the trailer, George was whinnying, but inside the barn, Delilah was going crazy. She was whinnying and prancing around her stall. She seemed to know her friend was outside.

Piper walked George off the trailer and into the barn. She put him in the stall next to Delilah. The two pony friends touched noses to greet each other. Delilah nickered. She was so happy to have her friend with her.

As George got settled in his stall, Delilah walked over to her grain bucket and licked it clean.

"Delilah seems to be feeling much better," Miss Kari said, walking over to meet George.

"She was better the minute she heard George's whinny," Ruby told her.

"Maybe she was just missing her friend," Miss Kari mused.

Ruby thought about it. She thought about how lonely she had been the first night of camp. She thought about being homesick and missing her parents. She realized that Delilah might have been feeling lonely, too. She didn't have a horse next to her stall. She didn't have a pony friend in her paddock yesterday. Maybe Delilah had been feeling a little homesick, just like Ruby!

"Were you lonely and homesick, my girl?" Ruby asked Delilah. "Do you feel better now that George is here?"

Delilah rubbed her head on Ruby's arm. She seemed to say that she was feeling better.

Now that Delilah was feeling better and George was at camp, Ruby knew it was going to be the best week ever. She couldn't wait to go swimming with the ponies that afternoon.

"Thanks, Mom and Dad," Ruby thought to herself, "for sending me to this awesome camp with my pony and our best friends!"

The Ugly Pony

Jada, Colette, and Miles all rushed into the barn. Today was the day the new ponies arrived! What would they look like? Would they be sweet or sassy? Would they be fun to ride?

Every spring, the barn owner, Mrs. Helen, would go to her friend's farm and pick out new ponies for the riding school. Sometimes her friend had retired show ponies that needed a break from showing. Sometimes she had young ponies that needed a little more experience. It was always exciting to see the new ponies as they arrived at the farm. Some of the ponies would stay for a while and then get sold to new homes so they could have a special person. Other times, the ponies stayed at Mrs. Helen's to be part of the riding lesson program.

Jada was excited because this year she had been chosen for a big job. Each spring, when the new ponies arrived, Mrs. Helen picked special riders who had been working hard and doing their best. These riders each got assigned to one of the new ponies. They got to care for the pony as if it were their own. They got to brush and ride the pony. Jada couldn't wait! She didn't have a pony of her own, so this was the next best thing.

Colette and Miles had also been chosen by Mrs. Helen. The three friends were excited to meet their ponies.

"Hello!" called Mrs. Helen in a big, booming voice. "Are you happy the new ponies are here? I got some great ones this time. I have one in particular that I think is extra special. Are you ready to meet them?"

"Yes!" The students all nodded at each other.

They walked to the back part of the barn that housed the new ponies.

"I only brought home three this time, but I think you will like all of them," Mrs. Helen paused outside the first stall. "This is Cloud. He was a jumper, but he needs a little time off. He will love doing riding lessons and trail rides, maybe even a little dressage."

"I love dressage! Can I be Cloud's partner? PLEASE!" Colette begged.

"I think that would be an ideal match," Mrs. Helen agreed. Colette squealed and went in to meet Cloud. Cloud was a lovely light gray with a few dapples. He had a flowing mane and tail. He whickered at Colette as she approached him.

"Next, we have a young pony. He will need a confident rider who is brave."

Miles raised his hand. Miles had been riding the longest of any of them. He was definitely a brave rider.

"Miles, meet Salsa. He is a spicy pony!" Mrs. Helen laughed. Salsa was a handsome bay. He had a shiny coat and a cute, crooked blaze on his face. He shook his head up and down when Miles went into the stall.

Mrs. Helen turned to Jada. "Well, I think this worked out just as I had hoped. I've got a special pony for you. You are a hard worker and just the kind of rider this pony needs. His name is Swan. Give him some time, and I think he will live up to his name."

Jada wasn't sure what Mrs. Helen meant. She peered into the dark stall. A shaggy, skinny pony hung out in the back of the stall. He didn't come over to greet Jada. He barely glanced at her.

Jada was confused. Her friends had been given beautiful, friendly ponies to play with. Swan was not beautiful or friendly. He was pretty ugly. He seemed tired and dull.

Still, an ugly, dull pony was better than no pony at all. Jada decided she had to make the best of it. She pulled a carrot out of her pocket and went over to Swan. He gently lipped at the carrot and gave Jada a shy bump with his nose. Maybe he did want to be friends!

Jada looked the pony over. His coat was very shaggy, as if he were ready for a blizzard. It was so overgrown that it was difficult to tell what color he was. It was an odd combination of brown and orange. His mane and tail were long and full of knots. His feet were overgrown. He was kind of skinny. Overall, he did not look like a champion show pony.

"I've got my work cut out for me," she said to herself.

Colette and Miles came up to the stall.

"You should see Cloud! He is the most beautiful pony," Colette bragged.

"Salsa has the best personality. He is such a clown. It's going to be so fun to work with him," Miles went on.

They both peered at Swan.

"Wow, this pony needs some work," Colette grimaced.

Miles just looked at the pony with a sad expression on his face.

"Don't worry. I'm going to turn this pony into something special. Just you wait and see," Jada told them.

Her friends nodded, trying to make her feel better. But she could see the relief on their faces that they had been assigned the beautiful, friendly ponies, while she got the ugly one.

True to her word, Jada got to work. Over the next few weeks, she spent every free moment in the barn. She gained Swan's trust with cookies. (Oatmeal cookies were his favorite.) He needed to gain weight, so Mrs. Helen had Jada feeding him a special diet. She couldn't ride Swan yet. Mrs. Helen wanted him to be a little more settled. So Jada spent lots of time letting him graze on fresh grass near the arena. Colette and Miles often rode their ponies while she grazed Swan. Their ponies seemed very nice. Cloud looked so smooth when he trotted and Salsa was a great jumper. Jada was a little jealous. She wished she was able to ride, too.

Jada overheard Colette talking one day, "I'm so glad Mrs. Helen gave me Cloud to ride. Poor Jada got such an ugly pony. Cloud is beautiful."

Jada wanted to cry. She was starting to really like Swan. He was sweet, in a shy kind of way, but Jada could tell Swan loved and trusted her.

When the weather warmed up, Mrs. Helen helped Jada body clip Swan's overgrown coat. They used clippers to shave off all the shaggy fur and leave only the short, shiny hair underneath.

"I'll bet you feel better," Jada told Swan as she finished clipping. Underneath all the hair, Swan had a beautiful coat. It was dark brown, almost black. His tall white socks gleamed with all of the mud finally gone. Jada had spent hours brushing through his mane and tail. She removed all the knots and trimmed it so it was tidy. The farrier had come and trimmed his hooves, so they looked healthy again.

When she stood back to admire the newly clipped pony, Jada couldn't believe what she saw. Swan did not look ugly anymore. He was beautiful. With the special diet, he had really blossomed. He was no longer skinny. His coat, mane, and tail were shiny and trimmed. He looked special! Jada might even say he was one of the most beautiful horses in the barn.

As she led him out to graze, she passed Colette and Cloud getting ready to ride.

"Wow, who is that?!" Colette asked as Swan walked by.

"It's Swan. Don't you recognize him?" Jada teased.

Colette's mouth dropped open in surprise. "Are you sure? He doesn't look like the same pony."

Jada held out an oatmeal cookie that Swan quickly inhaled. "Oh, I'm sure!" she laughed. "I've never seen another horse that loves oatmeal cookies as much as Swan."

Finally, Jada had permission to ride Swan. Mrs. Helen said he was strong enough. Jada was a little nervous. It had taken so long to build his trust and make him into the beautiful pony that stood in front of her. Jada assumed Swan didn't have much training. She figured she had lots more work ahead of her.

With Mrs. Helen's help Jada rode Swan around the arena. First came the walk. It was smooth and Swan seemed to understand the simple directions. Turning, steering, and stopping all came easily.

"But will the trot be as easy?" Jada asked herself as she prepared to do a little more.

She cued for a trot, and Swan moved forward gracefully. He seemed like he knew what he was doing. He behaved like a well-trained pony.

"Looking good, Jada!" Miles encouraged as Jada prepared to canter Swan. Swan had a big, smooth canter. It was like sitting on a rocking horse. He just seemed to glide underneath her.

Jada was grinning when she finished riding. She had not been expecting that. She had been prepared to have months of work before Swan was well trained.

"He looks really fun!" Miles said.

Jada smiled. She was proud of Swan and their work together.

Later, in Mrs. Helen's office Jada finally asked, "Why did you assign Swan to me?"

Mrs. Helen laughed. "That little ugly pony? I'm sure you probably thought I didn't like you anymore! But it was the opposite. You are such a hard worker and a good rider. I knew Swan would thrive with you as his person. Remember the first day? I said I had one pony that I thought was very special. It was Swan!"

"But how did you know he would turn out like this?"

"Have you ever heard of the story of the Ugly Duckling? A little duckling is born. He spends a long time feeling out of place because he doesn't look like the other ducks. They called him ugly. But it turns out he is not a duck at all. When he grew up, he was a beautiful swan."

"That's why you named him Swan," Jada concluded.

"Yep! I knew he would be special, with a little hard work. You see, Swan was a champion show pony. My friend recognized him at an auction. He was in bad shape, but we knew he could be fixed. Now, we have a special pony and Swan has a wonderful life. I'd say that's a happy ending to the story, wouldn't you?"

Jada nodded.

Mrs. Helen continued, "I think it's important not to judge people or ponies by what they look like. It's better to see how much heart they have."

Jada grinned, "Thanks for picking me to be Swan's person. I'm so glad you did!"

The Horse Show

Amelia was excited for the horse show. She loved the chance to spend time with her pony and her friends. Her pony, Cupcake, had been riding so well at home. She just knew it was going to be a great weekend.

"Amelia, Amelia!" she heard someone calling as she walked Cupcake across the stable area.

Amelia looked around. She saw her friend Kenzie waving to her. Kenzie was letting her pony, Twilight, graze on a patch of grass. She waved to her and walked over to say hello.

"Are you excited to show this weekend?" Kenzie asked.

"Yep!" Amelia smiled. "I can't wait. What about you? Is Twilight ready?"

Kenzie nodded. "Twilight is such a good pony. She's always ready. My mom said the judge is really nice."

"Oh, good! Last year I didn't like the judge. She didn't like me or Cupcake! I think we placed last in every single class!"

"Well, I know you've been working really hard since then, and you've gotten a lot better. I don't think you have to worry about that happening at this show," Kenzie encouraged her friend.

"As long as we don't have that judge, I think we'll be great!" Amelia said.

The girls made plans to go get their horses ready and go for a practice ride in the arena. Amelia wanted to be sure that Cupcake got to see anything that might be scary. Horses like to have the time to settle in at a new place. They like to make sure they feel safe. Amelia always wanted to be sure that Cupcake felt safe. That way she could always do her best work.

The next morning, Amelia woke up bright and early. She was ready for the day. At the horse show, she fed Cupcake her breakfast. She made sure she was sparkling clean by giving her a good grooming. Amelia had given Cupcake a bath the day before, but she still used a wet towel to scrub any of the fur that seemed dirty. Amelia used a brush to comb through Cupcake's mane and tail, leaving them nice and silky. She worked her mane into beautiful braids. Finally, as the finishing touch, Amelia added hoof oil to Cupcake's hooves to make sure they were sparkling, too. She stood back and admired her work.

"Cupcake, you look beautiful!" Amelia told her proudly.

"Your pony looks ready, but I don't know about you," Amelia's mom laughed.

Amelia looked down. She was covered in horse hair and dirt. She had hoof oil on her fingers and hay in her hair. Amelia laughed, too.

"I guess I need to get polished up so I can show. I can't have my pony looking better than me!"

Amelia went to the camper to change clothes. She put on her riding pants and shirt. She brushed her hair and put it into a tidy bun. She scrubbed the dirt off her face and looked into the mirror and smiled. It was going to be a great day!

As she stepped out the door, Amelia put on her freshly polished boots. They were so shiny that she could almost see her reflection.

Amelia got Cupcake all tacked up with her polished saddle and bridle. She knew that she had done everything she could to look sharp for the judge today. All that was left to do was to show her horse.

Amelia listened in her first class as the riders were asked to walk, trot, and canter. She made sure she paid attention to the other riders around her. She didn't want any other horses to get too close to Cupcake. That made Cupcake nervous.

Cupcake was a good girl. She listened to everything Amelia told her and did it without fuss. Amelia was super proud when they called her for a 1st place ribbon.

"Wow, you're off to a great start!" her mom said as she fastened the blue ribbon to Cupcake's bridle for a picture.

Throughout the day, Amelia and Cupcake won lots of ribbons. When she sat down with Kenzie to eat lunch, each girl had an impressive pile of colorful ribbons to display on their stalls.

The last class was dressage. Amelia had to do a pattern in front of the judge. The judge scored each step of the pattern, and later she would receive a final score. Amelia liked dressage, but sometimes it made her nervous to be the only rider in the arena. She felt like everyone was watching her! She had been working really hard all winter to get better at the pattern. Still, she felt like dressage was her hardest class of the day.

When Amelia was done with dressage, she rode out of the ring with a smile on her face. She had a few things she could do better tomorrow, but she was happy with how the ride went. She was even happier when it was announced that she had placed fourth in her dressage class.

"All your hard work is paying off," Amelia's mom told her as she helped her untack Cupcake. "You set some big goals, and you've worked hard to make them happen. I'm proud of you!"

"Thanks, Mom!" Amelia said as she gave Cupcake a kiss on the nose.

Amelia was much more tired on the second day of the horse show. Still, she got up and got to work getting Cupcake ready for the day. She was in the stall brushing her when Kenzie walked over.

"Did you hear about the judge?" Kenzie asked.

"No, what about her?"

"The judge got sick and can't come today. They had to find someone to replace her. They got Jennifer French to come and judge," Kenzie wrinkled her nose. "She's the judge from last year."

Amelia's heart sank. She had been looking forward to another great day of winning ribbons. Now, she just felt sad.

"She really didn't like Cupcake and me last year," Amelia gulped. "I felt like we couldn't do anything right."

As Amelia turned back to brush Cupcake, she wondered if it was even worth showing today. She told her mom what had happened when her mom came in to help.

"Maybe we should just go home now. I'm tired, and I'm sure Cupcake is tired, too. I don't want to hang around all day and get last place in all my classes," Amelia said sadly.

Amelia's mom frowned. "That sounds like quitting. You don't know how you are going to do this year. You have worked really hard to improve from last year. Don't you think you owe it to Cupcake to go in there and give it a try? Cupcake is a good pony!"

Amelia glared. "But the judge doesn't like us!"

"Maybe she didn't like you last year. But you are a much better rider now than you were last year. You owe it to yourself and your horse to give it a try."

"Fine, I'll try," Amelia grumbled, but she didn't feel very hopeful.

As Amelia was finishing up getting Cupcake ready to show, Cupcake nudged Amelia's arm. She stuck her muzzle to Amelia's face as if giving her a kiss. Then she rested her head on Amelia's shoulder. She seemed to be saying, "We can do this. We are a team."

Amelia felt bad. She trusted her pony. Cupcake was the best pony! She deserved the chance to show this judge what she could do.

"Okay, girl," Amelia said. "Let's give this our best shot."

Amelia trotted into the ring. She was confident and proud. Cupcake looked proud, too. They walked, trotted, and cantered with style. It was a great ride. As

Amelia waited for the results, she didn't care what the judge thought. Cupcake had given her a great ride, and that was the most important thing.

"First place to Amelia Grant riding Cupcake!" the announcer called.

Amelia's face broke into a huge smile. She gave Cupcake a giant pat as she rode over to get her ribbon.

"Nice ride!" the judge told her.

"Thank you!" Amelia replied, still grinning.

The rest of the day, Amelia and Cupcake won either first or second place in all of their classes. It was her best show yet. Amelia was happy they had decided to stay and show. Her mom was right; she had worked hard over the winter. She was a much better rider than she was last year.

When it was time for the last ride of the day, the dressage class, Amelia went into the ring with a smile. She and Cupcake had fun doing the pattern. Amelia just focused on doing her best.

When she finished, the judge called her over.

"Wow, that was a beautiful ride! All day long, you and your pony have performed so well. You look like you are having fun together. That is the most important thing," Miss French said.

"We've been working really hard," Amelia told her.

"I can tell. I remember you from last year. You had a few things to work on, but you worked hard and look at you now! You should feel proud of yourself. You are an excellent rider and you take good care of your horse. I think you will have lots of blue ribbons in your future," Miss French encouraged.

Amelia thanked her. That compliment was better than any blue ribbon.

"I'm glad I stuck around and decided to show today," she told her mom as they walked back to the barn. "I'm glad we didn't quit when things weren't going our way. All that hard work was worth it!"

About the Author

Shannon Jett realized she was a horse crazy girl after her first riding lesson that she got for her 13th birthday. Her passion has given her the opportunity to observe many aspects of the equestrian world. Early on in her career she fell in love with the Arabian horse. She's been lucky enough to train two National Champion Arabians.

Shannon currently lives in Tennessee with her husband, two daughters, dog, cat, and a stable full of horses. If she's not riding or writing, she's probably cleaning stalls.

Made in the USA
Middletown, DE
14 December 2024